She went to bed and pulled the duvet

up to meet her chin,

switched off the light and fell asleep,

all tidily tucked in.

Then Miffy Bunny had a dream

which made her feel so grand.

She dreamed she was the Queen of Rabbits

ruling Rabbit Land.

Her home was now a palace

with walls of gleaming white.

A royal flag flew high above.

It was a pretty sight.

Her loyal rabbit subjects

adored their lovely queen.

They smiled and cheered and waved to her

whenever she was seen.

Miffy always waved right back.

That's why it was agreed

that having such a special queen

was great good luck indeed.

On any fine occasion

as Queen she would appear

to cut the coloured ribbons.

Then everyone would cheer.

But if some sad thing happened

to make a rabbit cry

Queen Miffy would bring comfort

and help their tears to dry.

Queen Miffy read through all the post

she regularly got.

She busily sent letters back

and often wrote a lot.

Every year her people

would plant a new young tree.

A birthday present for their queen

that everyone could see.

The rabbits then would wave their flags

and sing, hip, hip, hooray!

Long live our good Queen Miffy.

This is her special day.

And then, the dream was over.

What a shame it was so short.

But being Queen was thrilling.

That's what Miffy thought.